For my wild little ones.

Emma and Snowbell

by Mary Lee

Pushing through the snow,
Emma could really use a sled.

She's stuck and cannot go,

so she finds a ride instead.

Bells on the reindeer ring,

making Emma smile.

What fun it is to ride and sing,
and do it all in style.

Oh, Snowy Bells, Snowy Bells
Snowing all the way.

Oh, what fun it is to ride
a reindeer without a sleigh.

From high up in the sky,

Emma sees her school down there.

She calls out, "want to fly?"

And soon her class is in the air.

Oh, Snowy Bells, Snowy Bells,
Snowing all the way.

Oh, what fun it is to ride
a reindeer without a sleigh.

Santa's Workshop

Now it's getting late. Santa is almost here.

Emma needs to get to bed.
Soon her presents will appear.

So goodnight, Snowbell.
Goodnight to all your friends.

Have a wonderful Noel.
This story is near it's end.

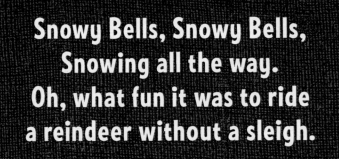

Snowy Bells, Snowy Bells,
Snowing all the way.
Oh, what fun it was to ride
a reindeer without a sleigh.

Snowy Bells, Snowy Bells,
Snowing all the way.
Oh, what fun it was to ride
a reindeer without a sleigh.

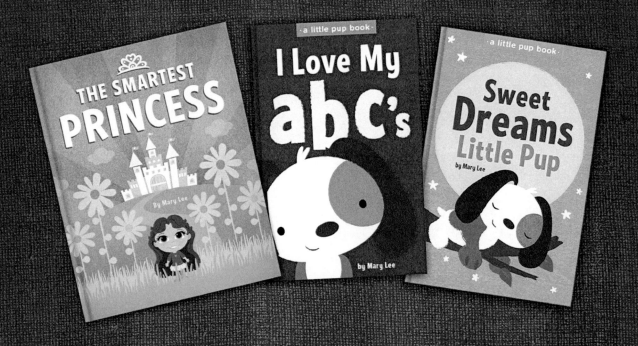

Find more books by Mary Lee at
www.maryleekids.blogspot.com

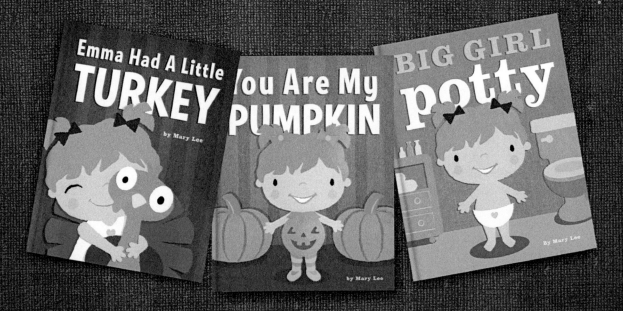

Made in the USA
Middletown, DE
18 December 2014